FAUST

INCLUDING THE ILLUSTRATED ESSAY 'A NOTE ON LITERATURE'

by

IVAN TURGENEV

D1523659

COMPASS CIRCLE

Faust.
Written by Ivan Turgenev.
Translated by Constance Garnett.
Current edition published by Compass Circle in 2022.

Published by Compass Circle
Cover copyright ©2022 by Compass Circle.

Note:
All efforts have been made to preserve original spellings and punctuation of the original edition which may include old-fashioned English spellings of words and archaic variants.

This book is a product of its time and does not reflect the same views on race, gender, sexuality, ethnicity, and interpersonal relations as it would if it were written today.

For information contact :
information@compass-circle.com

We sit in the mud, my friend, and reach for the stars.

IVAN TURGENEV

SECRET WISDOM OF THE AGES SERIES

Life presents itself, it advances in a fast way. Life indeed never stops. It never stops until the end. The most diverse questions peek and fade in our minds. Sometimes we seek for answers. Sometimes we just let time go by.

The book you have now in your hands has been waiting to be discovered by you. This book may reveal the answers to some of your questions.

Books are friends. Friends who are always by your side and who can give you great ideas, advice or just comfort your soul.

A great book can make you see things in your soul that you have not yet discovered, make you see things in your soul that you were not aware of.

Great books can change your life for the better. They can make you understand fascinating theories, give you new ideas, inspire you to undertake new challenges or to walk along new paths.

Literature Classics like the one of *Faust* are indeed a secret to many, but for those of us lucky enough to have discovered them, by one way or another, these books can enlighten us. They can open a wide range of possibilities to us. Because achieving greatness requires knowledge.

The series SECRET WISDOM OF THE AGES presented by Compass Circle try to bring you the great timeless masterpieces of literature, autobiographies and personal development,.

We welcome you to discover with us fascinating works by Nathaniel Hawthorne, Sir Arthur Conan Doyle, Edith Wharton, among others.

Contents

IVAN TURGENEV

Born   Ivan Sergeyevich Turgenev
November 9, 1818
Oryol, Russia

Died   September 3, 1883
Bougival, France

IVAN TURGENEV

FAUST

A STORY IN NINE LETTERS

Entbehren sollst du, sollst entbehren

(Faust, Part I.)

First Letter

FROM PAVEL ALEXANDROVITCH B.... TO SEMYON NIKOLAEVITCH V....

M—— Village, *6th June 1850*.

I HAVE been here for three days, my dear fellow, and, as I promised, I take up my pen to write to you. It has been drizzling with fine rain ever since the morning; I can't go out; and I want a little chat with you, too. Here I am again in my old home, where—it's a dreadful thing to say—I have not been for nine long years. Really, as you may fancy, I have become quite a different man. Yes, utterly different, indeed; do you remember, in the drawing-room, the little tarnished looking-glass of my great-grandmother's, with the queer little curly scrolls in the corners—you always used to be speculating on what it had seen a hundred years ago—directly I arrived, I went up to it, and I could not help feeling disconcerted. I suddenly saw how old and changed I had become in these last

3

years. But I am not alone in that respect. My little house, which was old and tottering long ago, will hardly hold together now, it is all on the slant, and seems sunk into the ground. My dear Vassilievna, the housekeeper (you can't have forgotten her; she used to regale you with such capital jam), is quite shrivelled up and bent; when she saw me, she could not call out, and did not start crying, but only moaned and choked, sank helplessly into a chair, and waved her hand. Old Terenty has some spirit left in him still; he holds himself up as much as ever, and turns out his feet as he walks. He still wears the same yellow nankeen breeches, and the same creaking goatskin slippers, with high heels and ribbons, which touched you so much sometimes, ... but, mercy on us!—how the breeches flap about his thin legs nowadays! how white his hair has grown! and his face has shrunk up into a sort of little fist. When he speaks to me, when he begins directing the servants, and giving orders in the next room, it makes me laugh and feel sorry for him. All his teeth are gone, and he mumbles with a whistling, hissing sound. On the other hand, the garden has got on wonderfully. The modest little plants of lilac, acacia, and honeysuckle (do you remember, we planted them together?) have grown into splendid, thick bushes. The birches, the maples—all that has spread out and grown tall; the avenues of lime-trees are particularly fine. I love those avenues, I love the tender grey, green colour, and the delicate fragrance of the air under their arching boughs; I love the changing net-work of rings of light on the dark earth—there is no sand here, you know. My favourite oak sapling has grown into a young oak tree. Yesterday I spent more than an hour in the middle of the day on a garden bench in its shade. I felt very happy. All about me the grass was deliciously luxuriant; a rich, soft, golden light lay upon everything; it made its way even into the shade ... and the birds one could hear! You've not forgotten, I expect, that birds are a passion of mine? The turtle-doves cooed unceasingly; from time to time there came the whistle of the oriole; the chaffinch uttered its sweet little refrain; the blackbirds quarrelled and twittered; the cuckoo called far away; suddenly, like a mad thing, the woodpecker uttered its shrill cry. I listened and listened to this subdued, mingled sound, and did not want to move, while my heart was full of something between languor and tenderness.

And it's not only the garden that has grown up: I am continually coming across sturdy, thick-set lads, whom I cannot recognise as the little boys I used to know in old days. Your favourite, Timosha, has turned into a Timofay, such as you could never imagine. You had fears in those days for his health, and predicted consumption; but now you should just see his huge, red hands, as they stick out from the narrow sleeves of his nankeen coat, and the stout rounded muscles that stand out all over him! He has a neck like a bull's, and a head all over tight, fair curls—a regular Farnese Hercules. His face, though, has changed less than the others'; it is not even much larger in circumference, and the good-humoured, 'gaping'—as you used to say—smile has remained the same. I have taken him to be my valet; I got rid of my Petersburg fellow at Moscow; he was really too fond of putting me to shame, and making me feel the superiority of his Petersburg manners. Of my dogs I have not found one; they have all passed away. Nefka lived longer than any of them—and she did not live till my return, as Argos lived till the return of Ulysses; she was not fated to look once more with her lustreless eyes on her master and companion in the chase. But Shavka is all right, and barks as hoarsely as ever, and has one ear torn just the same, and burrs sticking to his tail,—all just as it should be. I have taken up my abode in what was your room. It is true the sun beats down upon it, and there are a lot of flies in it; but there is less of the smell of the old house in it than in the other rooms. It's a queer thing; that musty, rather sour, faint smell has a powerful effect on my imagination; I don't mean that it's disagreeable to me, quite the contrary, but it produces melancholy, and, at last, depression. I am very fond, just as you are, of podgy old chests with brass plates, white armchairs with oval backs, and crooked legs, fly-blown glass lustres, with a big egg of lilac tinsel in the centre—of all sorts of ancestral furniture, in fact. But I can't stand seeing it all continually; a sort of agitated dejection (it is just that) takes possession of me. In the room where I have established myself, the furniture is of the most ordinary, home-made description. I have left, though, in the corner, a long narrow set of shelves, on which there is an old-fashioned set of blown green and blue glasses, just discernible through the dust. And I have had hung on the wall that portrait of a woman—you remember, in the black frame?—that you used to call the portrait of Manon Lescaut. It has got rather darker in these nine years; but the eyes have the same pensive, sly, and tender look, the lips have the same capricious, melancholy smile, and the half-plucked rose falls as softly as ever from her slender fingers. I am greatly amused by the blinds in my room. They were once green, but have been turned yellow by the sun; on them are depicted, in dark colours, scenes from d'Arlencourt's *Hermit.* On one curtain the hermit, with an immense beard, goggle-eyes, and sandals on his feet, is carrying off a young lady with dishevelled locks to the mountains. On another one, there is a terrific combat going on between four knights wearing birettas, and with puffs on their shoulders; one, much foreshortened, lies slain—in fact, there are pictures of all sorts of horrors, while all about there is such unbroken peace, and the blinds themselves throw such soft light on the ceiling.... A sort of inward calm has come upon me since I have been settled here; one wants to do nothing, one wants to see no one, one looks forward to nothing, one is too lazy for thought, but not too lazy for musing; two different things, as you know well. Memories of childhood, at first, came flooding upon me—wherever I went, whatever I looked at, they surged up on all sides, distinct, to the smallest detail, and, as it were, immovable, in their clearly defined outlines.... Then these memories were succeeded by others, then ... then I gradually turned away from the past, and all that was left was a sort of drowsy heaviness in my heart. Fancy! as I was sitting on the dike, under a willow, I suddenly and unexpectedly burst out crying, and should have gone on crying a long while, in spite of my advanced years, if I had not been put to shame by a passing peasant woman, who stared at me with curiosity, then, without turning her face towards me, gave a low bow from the waist, and passed on. I should be very glad to remain in the same mood (I shan't do any more crying, of course) till I go away from here; that is, till September, and should be very sorry if any of my neighbours should take it into his head to call on me. However there is no danger, I fancy, of that; I have no near neighbours here. You will understand me, I'm sure; you know yourself, by experience, how often solitude is beneficial ... I need it now after wanderings of all sorts.

But I shan't be dull. I have brought a few books with me, and I have a pretty fair library here. Yesterday, I opened all the bookcases, and was a long while rummaging about among the musty books. I found many curious things I had not noticed before: *Candide*, in a manuscript translation of somewhere about 1770; newspapers and magazines of the same period;

the Triumphant Chameleon (that is, Mirabeau), *le Paysan Perverti*, etc. I came across children's books, my own, and my father's, and my grandmother's, and even, fancy, my great grandmother's; in one dilapidated French grammar in a particoloured binding, was written in fat letters: 'Ce livre appartient à Mlle Eudoxie de Lavrine,' and it was dated 1741. I saw books I had brought at different times from abroad, among others, Goethe's *Faust*. You're not aware, perhaps, that there was a time when I knew *Faust* by heart (the first part, of course) word for word; I was never tired of reading it.... But other days, other dreams, and for the last nine years, it has so happened, that I have scarcely had a Goethe in my hand. It was with an indescribable emotion that I saw the little book I knew so well, again (a poor edition of 1828). I brought it away with me, lay down on the bed, and began to read. How all that splendid first scene affected me! The entrance of the Spirit of the Earth, the words, you remember—'on the tide of life, in the whirl of creation,' stirred a long unfamiliar tremor and shiver of ecstasy. I recalled everything: Berlin, and student days, and Fräulein Clara Stick, and Zeidelmann in the *rôle* of Mephistopheles, and the music of Radzivil, and all and everything.... It was a long while before I could get to sleep: my youth rose up and stood before me like a phantom; it ran like fire, like poison through my veins, my heart leaped and would not be still, something plucked at its chords, and yearnings began surging up....

You see what fantasies your friend gives himself up to, at almost forty, when he sits in solitude in his solitary little house! What if any one could have peeped at me! Well, what? I shouldn't have been a bit ashamed of myself. To be ashamed is a sign of youth, too; and I have begun (do you know how?) to notice that I'm getting old. I'll tell you how. I try in these days to make as much as I can of my happy sensations, and to make little of my sad ones, and in the days of my youth I did just the opposite. At times, one used to carry about one's melancholy as if it were a treasure, and be ashamed of a cheerful mood.... But for all that, it strikes me, that in spite of all my experience of life, there is something in the world, friend Horatio, which I have not experienced, and that 'something' almost the most important.

Oh, what have I worked myself up to! Farewell for the present! What are you about in Petersburg? By the way; Savely, my country cook, wishes to send his duty to you. He too is older, but not very much so, he is grown rather corpulent, stouter all over. He is as good as ever at chicken-soup, with stewed onions, cheesecakes with goffered edges, and peagoose— peagoose is the famous dish of the steppes, which makes your tongue white and rough for twenty-four hours after. On the other hand, he roasts the meat as he always did, so that you can hammer on the plate with it—hard as a board. But I must really say, good-bye!

Yours, P. B.

Second Letter

From the SAME to the SAME

M—— Village, *June 12, 1850*.

I HAVE rather an important piece of news to tell you, my dear friend. Listen! Yesterday I felt disposed for a walk before dinner—only not in the garden; I walked along the road towards the town. Walking rapidly, quite aimlessly, along a straight, long road is very pleasant. You feel as if you're doing something, hurrying somewhere. I look up; a coach is coming towards me. Surely not some one to see me, I wondered with secret terror.... No: there was a gentleman with moustaches in the carriage, a stranger to me. I felt reassured. But all of a sudden, when he got abreast with me, this gentleman told the coachman to stop the horses, politely raised his cap, and still more politely asked me, 'was not I ...' mentioning my name. I too came to a standstill, and with the fortitude of a prisoner brought up for trial, replied that I was myself; while I stared like a sheep at the gentleman with the moustaches and said to myself—'I do believe I've seen him somewhere!'

'You don't recognise me?' he observed, as he got out of the coach.

'No, I don't.'

'But I knew you directly.'

Explanations followed; it appeared that it was Priemkov—do you remember?—a fellow we used to know at the university. 'Why, is that an important piece of news?' you are asking yourself at this instant, my dear Semyon Nikolaitch. 'Priemkov, to the best of my recollection, was rather a dull chap; no harm in him though, and not a fool.' Just so, my dear boy; but hear the rest of our conversation.

'I was delighted,' says he, 'when I heard you had come to your country-place, into our neighbourhood. But I was not alone in that feeling.'

'Allow me to ask,' I questioned: 'who was so kind....'

'My wife.'

'Your wife!'

'Yes, my wife; she is an old acquaintance of yours.'

'May I ask what was your wife's name?'

'Vera Nikolaevna; she was an Eltsov....'

'Vera Nikolaevna!' I could not help exclaiming....

This it is, which is the important piece of news I spoke of at the beginning of my letter.

But perhaps you don't see anything important even in this.... I shall have to tell you something of my past ... long past, life.

When we both left the university in 183— I was three-and-twenty. You went into the service; I decided, as you know, to go to Berlin. But there was nothing to be done in Berlin before October. I wanted to spend the summer in Russia—in the country—to have a good lazy holiday for the last time; and then to set to work in earnest. How far this last project was carried out, there is no need to enlarge upon here ...
'But where am I to spend the summer?' I asked myself. I did not want to go to my own place; my father

had died not long before, I had no near relations, I was afraid of the solitude and dreariness.... And so I was delighted to receive an invitation from a distant cousin to stay at his country-place in T ... province. He was a well-to-do, good-natured, simple-hearted man; he lived in style as a country magnate, and had a palatial country house. I went to stay there. My cousin had a large family; two sons and five daughters. Besides them, there was always a crowd of people in his house. Guests were for ever arriving; and yet it wasn't jolly at all. The days were spent in noisy entertainments, there was no chance of being by oneself. Everything was done in common, every one tried to be entertaining, to invent some amusement, and at the end of the day every one was fearfully exhausted. There was something vulgar about the way we lived. I was already beginning to look forward to getting away, and was only waiting till my cousin's birthday festivities were over, when on the very day of those festivities, at the ball, I saw Vera Nikolaevna Eltsov—and I stayed on.

She was at that time sixteen. She was living with her mother on a little estate four miles from my cousin's place. Her father—a remarkable man, I have been told—had risen rapidly to the grade of colonel, and would have attained further distinctions, but he died young, accidentally shot by a friend when out shooting. Vera Nikolaevna was a baby at the time of his death. Her mother too was an exceptional woman; she spoke several languages, and was very well informed. She was seven or eight years older than her husband whom she had married for love; he had run away with her in secret from her father's house. She never got over his loss, and, till the day of her death (I heard from Priemkov that she had died soon after her daughter's marriage), she never wore anything but black. I have a vivid recollection of her face: it was expressive, dark, with thick hair beginning to turn grey; large, severe, lustreless eyes, and a straight, fine nose. Her father—his surname was Ladanov—had lived for fifteen years in Italy. Vera Nikolaevna's mother was the daughter of a simple Albanian peasant girl, who, the day after giving birth to her child, was killed by her betrothed lover—a Transteverino peasant—from whom Ladanov had enticed her away.... The story made a great sensation at the time. On his return to Russia, Ladanov never left his house, nor even his study; he devoted himself to chemistry, anatomy, and magical arts; tried to discover means to prolong human life, fancied he could hold intercourse with spirits, and call up the dead.... The neighbours looked upon him as a sorcerer. He was extremely fond of his daughter, and taught her everything himself: but he never forgave her elopement with Eltsov, never allowed either of them to come into his presence, predicted a life of sorrow for both of them, and died in solitude. When Madame Eltsov was left a widow, she devoted her whole time to the education of her daughter, and scarcely saw any friends. When I first met Vera Nikolaevna, she had—just fancy—never been in a town in her life, not even in the town of her district.

Vera Nikolaevna was not like the common run of Russian girls; there was the stamp of something special upon her. I was struck from the first minute by the extraordinary repose of all her movements and remarks. She seemed free from any sort of disturbance or agitation; she answered simply and intelligently, and listened attentively. The expression of her face was sincere and truthful as a child's, but a little cold and immobile, though not dreamy. She was rarely gay, and not in the way other girls are; the serenity of an innocent heart shone out in everything about her, and cheered one more than any gaiety. She was not tall, and had a very good figure, rather slender; she had soft, regular features, a lovely smooth brow, light golden hair, a straight nose, like her mother's, and rather full lips; her dark grey eyes looked out somewhat too directly from under soft, upward-turned eyelashes. Her hands were small, and not very pretty; one never sees hands like hers on people of talent ... and, as a fact, Vera Nikolaevna had no special talents. Her voice rang out clear as a child of seven's. I was presented to her mother at my cousin's ball, and a few days later I called on them for the first time.

Madame Eltsov was a very strange woman, a woman of character, of strong will and concentration. She had a great influence on me; I at once respected her and feared her. Everything with her was done on a principle, and she had educated her daughter too on a principle, though she did not interfere with her freedom. Her daughter loved her and trusted her blindly. Madame Eltsov had only to give her a book, and say—'Don't read that page,' she would prefer to skip the preceding page as well, and would certainly never glance at the page interdicted. But Madame Eltsov too had her *idées fixes*, her fads. She was mortally afraid, for instance, of anything that might work upon the imagination. And so her daughter reached the age of seventeen without ever having read a novel or a poem, while in Geography, History, and even Natural History, she would often put me to shame, graduate as I was, and a graduate, as you know, not by any means low down on the list either. I used to try and argue with Madame Eltsov about her fad, though it was difficult to draw her into conversation; she was very silent. She simply shook her head.

'You tell me,' she said at last, 'that reading poetry is *both* useful *and* pleasant.... I consider one must make one's choice early in life; *either* the useful *or* the pleasant, and abide by it once for all. I, too, tried at one time to unite the two.... That's impossible, and leads to ruin or vulgarity.'

Yes, a wonderful being she was, that woman, an upright, proud nature, not without a certain fanaticism and superstition of her own. 'I am afraid of life,' she said to me one day. And really she was afraid of it, afraid of those secret forces on which life rests and which rarely, but so suddenly, break out. Woe to him who is their sport! These forces had shown themselves in fearful shape for Madame Eltsov; think of her mother's death, her husband's, her father's.... Any one would have been panic-stricken. I never saw her smile. She had, as it were, locked herself up and thrown the key into the water. She must have suffered great grief in her time, and had never shared it with any one; she had hidden it all away within herself. She had so thoroughly trained herself not to give way to her feelings that she was even ashamed to express her passionate love for her daughter; she never once kissed her in my presence, and never used any endearing names, always Vera. I remember one saying of hers; I happened to say to her that all of us modern people were half broken by life. 'It's no good being half broken,' she observed; 'one must be broken in thoroughly or let it alone....'

Very few people visited Madame Eltsov; but I went often to see her. I was secretly aware that she looked on me with favour; and I liked Vera Nikolaevna very much indeed. We used to talk and walk together.... Her mother was no check upon us; the daughter did not like to be away from her mother, and I, for my part, felt no craving for solitary talks with her.... Vera Nikolaevna had a strange habit of thinking aloud; she used at night in her sleep to talk loudly and distinctly about what had impressed her during the day. One day, looking at me attentively, leaning softly, as her way was, on her hand, she said, 'It seems to me that B. is a good person, but there's no relying on him.' The relations existing between us were of the friendliest and most tranquil; only once I fancied I detected somewhere far off in the very depths of her clear eyes something strange, a sort of softness and tenderness.... But perhaps I was mistaken.

Meanwhile the time was slipping by, and it was already time for me to prepare for departure. But still I put it off. At times, when I thought, when I realised that soon I should see no more of this sweet girl I had grown so fond of, I felt sick at heart.... Berlin began to lose its attractive force. I had not the courage to acknowledge to myself what was going on within me, and, indeed, I didn't understand what was taking place,—it was as though a cloud were overhanging my soul. At last one morning everything suddenly became clear to me. 'Why seek further, what is there to strive towards? Why, I shall not attain to truth in any case. Isn't it better to stay here, to be married?' And, imagine, the idea of marriage had no terrors for me in those days. On the contrary, I rejoiced in it. More than that; that day I declared my intentions; only not to Vera Nikolaevna, as one would naturally suppose, but to Madame Eltsov. The old lady looked at me.

'No,' she said; 'my dear boy, go to Berlin, get broken in thoroughly. You're a good fellow; but it's not a husband like you that's needed for Vera.'

I hung my head, blushed, and, what will very likely surprise you still more, inwardly agreed with Madame Eltsov on the spot. A week later I went away,

and since then I have not seen her nor Vera Nikolaevna.

I have related this episode briefly because I know
you don't care for anything 'meandering.' When I
got to Berlin I very quickly forgot Vera Nikolaevna....
But I will own that hearing of her so unexpectedly
has excited me. I am impressed by the idea that she
is so close, that she is my neighbour, that I shall see
her in a day or two. The past seems suddenly to have
sprung up out of the earth before my eyes, and to
have rushed down upon me. Priemkov informed me
that he was coming to call upon me with the very
object of renewing our old acquaintance, and that he
should look forward to seeing me at his house as soon
as I could possibly come. He told me he had been in
the cavalry, had retired with the rank of lieutenant,
had bought an estate about six miles from me, and
was intending to devote himself to its management,
that he had had three children, but that two had died,
and he had only a little girl of five surviving.

'And does your wife remember me?' I inquired.

'Yes, she remembers you,' he replied, with some
slight hesitation. 'Of course, she was a child, one
may say, in those days; but her mother always spoke
very highly of you, and you know how precious every
word of her poor mother's is to her.'

I recalled Madame Eltsov's words, that I was not
suitable for her Vera.... 'I suppose you were suitable,' I thought, with a sidelong look at Priemkov. He
spent some hours with me. He is a very nice, dear,

good fellow, speaks so modestly, and looks at me so good-naturedly. One can't help liking him … but his intellectual powers have not developed since we used to know him. I shall certainly go and see him, possibly to-morrow. I am exceedingly curious to see how Vera Nikolaevna has turned out.

You, spiteful fellow, are most likely laughing at me as you read this, sitting at your directors' table. But I shall write and tell you, all the same, the impression she makes on me. Good-bye—till my next.—

Yours, P. B.

Third Letter

From the SAME to the SAME

M——— Village, *June 16, 1850*.

WELL, my dear boy, I have been to her house; I have seen her. First of all I must tell you one astonishing fact: you may believe me or not as you like, but she has scarcely changed at all either in face or in figure. When she came to meet me, I almost cried out in amazement; it was simply a little girl of seventeen! Only her eyes are not a little girl's; but then her eyes were never like a child's, even in her young days,— they were too clear. But the same composure, the same serenity, the same voice, not one line on her brow, as though she had been laid in the snow all these years. And she's twenty-eight now, and has had three children.… It's incomprehensible! Don't imag- ine, please, that I had some preconceived preference,

and so am exaggerating; quite the other way; I don't
like this absence of change in her a bit.

A woman of eight-and-twenty, a wife and a mother,
ought not to be like a little girl; she should have
gained something from life. She gave me a very cor-
dial welcome; but Priemkov was simply overjoyed
at my arrival; the dear fellow seems on the look-out
for some one to make much of. Their house is very
cosy and clean. Vera Nikolaevna was dressed, too,
like a girl; all in white, with a blue sash, and a slender gold chain on her neck. Her daughter is very
sweet and not at all like her. She reminds one of
her grandmother. In the drawing-room, just over a
sofa, there hangs a portrait of that strange woman,
a striking likeness. It caught my eye directly I went
into the room. It seemed as though she were gazing
sternly and earnestly at me. We sat down, spoke of
old times, and by degrees got into conversation. I
could not help continually glancing at the gloomy
portrait of Madame Eltsov. Vera Nikolaevna was sitting just under it; it is her favourite place. Imagine
my amazement: Vera Nikolaevna has never yet read
a single novel, a single poem—in fact, not a single
invented work, as she expresses it! This incomprehensible indifference to the highest pleasures of the
intellect irritated me. In a woman of intelligence,
and as far as I can judge, of sensibility, it's simply
unpardonable.

'What? do you make it a principle,' I asked, 'never
to read books of that sort?'

'I have never happened to,' she answered; 'I haven't had time!'

'Not time! You surprise me! I should have thought,' I went on, addressing Priemkov, 'you would have interested your wife in poetry.'

'I should have been delighted——' Priemkov was beginning, but Vera Nikolaevna interrupted him—

'Don't pretend; you've no great love for poetry yourself.'

'Poetry; well, no,' he began; 'I'm not very fond of it; but novels, now....'

'But what do you do, how do you spend your evenings?' I queried; 'do you play cards?'

'We sometimes play,' she answered; 'but there's always plenty to do. We read, too; there are good books to read besides poetry.'

'Why are you so set against poetry?'

'I'm not set against it; I have been used to not reading these invented works from a child. That was my mother's wish, and the longer I live the more I am convinced that everything my mother did, everything she said, was right, sacredly right.'

'Well, as you will, but I can't agree with you; I am certain you are depriving yourself quite needlessly of the purest, the most legitimate pleasure. Why, you're not opposed to music and painting, I suppose; why be opposed to poetry?'

'I'm not opposed to it; I have never got to know anything of it—that's all.'

'Well, then, I will see to that! Your mother did not,

I suppose, wish to prevent your knowing anything of the works of creative, poetic art all your life?'

'No; when I was married, my mother removed every restriction; it never occurred to me to read—what did you call them?... well, anyway, to read novels.'

I listened to Vera Nikolaevna in astonishment. I had not expected this.

She looked at me with her serene glance. Birds look so when they are not frightened.

'I'll bring you a book!' I cried. (I thought of *Faust*, which I had just been reading.)

Vera Nikolaevna gave a gentle sigh.

'It———it won't be Georges—Sand?' she questioned with some timidity.

'Ah! then you've heard of her? Well, if it were, where's the harm?... No, I'll bring you another author. You've not forgotten German, have you?'

'No.'

'She speaks it like a German,' put in Priemkov.

'Well, that's splendid! I will bring you—but there, you shall see what a wonderful thing I will bring you.'

'Very good, we shall see. But now let us go into the garden, or there'll be no keeping Natasha still.'

She put on a round straw hat, a child's hat, just such a one as her daughter was wearing, only a little larger, and we went into the garden. I walked beside her. In the fresh air, in the shade of the tall limes, I thought her face looked sweeter than ever, especially when she turned a little and threw back her head so as to look up at me from under the brim of her hat. If it had not been for Priemkov walking behind us, and the little girl skipping about in front of us, I could really have fancied I was three-and-twenty, instead of thirty-five; and that I was just on the point of starting for Berlin, especially as the garden we were walking in was very much like the garden in Madame Eltsov's estate. I could not help expressing my feelings to Vera Nikolaevna.

'Every one tells me that I am very little changed externally,' she answered, 'though indeed I have remained just the same inwardly too.'

We came up to a little Chinese summer-house.

'We had no summer-house like this at Osinovka,' she said; 'but you mustn't mind its being so tumbledown and discoloured: it's very nice and cool inside.'

We went into the house. I looked round.

'I tell you what, Vera Nikolaevna,' I observed, 'you let them bring a table and some chairs in here. Here it is really delicious. I will read you here Goethe's *Faust*—that's the thing I am going to read you.'

'Yes, there are no flies here,' she observed simply. 'When will you come?'

'The day after to-morrow.'

'Very well,' she answered. 'I will arrange it.'

Natasha, who had come into the summer-house with us, suddenly gave a shriek and jumped back, quite pale.

'What is it?' inquired Vera Nikolaevna.

'O mammy,' said the little girl, pointing into the corner, 'look, what a dreadful spider!'

Vera Nikolaevna looked into the corner: a fat mottled spider was crawling slowly along the wall.

'What is there to fear in that?' she said. 'It won't bite, look.'

And before I had time to stop her, she took up the hideous insect, let it run over her hand, and threw it away.

'Well, you are brave!' I cried.

'Where is the bravery in that? It wasn't a venomous spider.'

'One can see you are as well up in Natural History as ever, but I couldn't have held it in my hand.'

'There's nothing to be afraid of!' repeated Vera Nikolaevna.

Natasha looked at us both in silence, and laughed.

'How like your mother she is!' I remarked.

'Yes,' rejoined Vera Nikolaevna with a smile of pleasure, 'it is a great happiness to me. God grant she may be like her, not in face only!'

We were called in to dinner, and after dinner I went away.

N.B.—The dinner was very good and well-cooked, an observation in parenthesis for you, you gourmand!

To-morrow I shall take them *Faust*. I'm afraid old Goethe and I may not come off very well. I will write and tell you all about it most exactly.

Well, and what do you think of all these proceedings? No doubt, that she has made a great impression on me, that I'm on the point of falling in love, and all the rest of it? Rubbish, my dear boy! There's a limit to everything. I've been fool enough. No more! One can't begin life over again at my age. Besides, I never did care for women of that sort.... Nice sort of women I did care for, if you come to that!!

'I shudder—my heart is sick—
I am ashamed of my idols.'

Any way, I am very glad of such neighbours, glad of the opportunity of seeing something of an intelligent, simple, bright creature. And as to what comes of it later on, you shall hear in due time.—

YOURS, P. B.

Fourth Letter

From the SAME to the SAME

M—— Village, *June 20, 1850*.

THE reading took place yesterday, dear friend, and here follows the manner thereof. First of all, I hasten to tell you: a success quite beyond all expectation—success, in fact, is not the word.... Well, I'll tell you. I arrived to dinner. We sat down a party of six to dinner: she, Priemkov, their little girl, the governess (an uninteresting colourless figure), I, and an old German in a short cinnamon-coloured frock-coat, very clean, well-shaved and brushed; he had the meekest, most honest face, and a toothless smile, and smelled of coffee mixed with chicory ... all old Germans have that peculiar odour about them. I was introduced to him; he was one Schimmel, a German tutor, living with the princes H., neighbours of the Priemkovs. Vera Nikolaevna, it appeared, had a liking for him, and had invited him to be present at the reading. We dined late, and sat a long while at table, and afterwards went a walk. The weather was exquisite. In the morning there had been rain and a blustering wind, but towards evening all was calm again. We came out on to an open meadow. Directly over the meadow a great rosy cloud poised lightly, high up in the sky; streaks of grey stretched like smoke over it; on its very edge, continually peeping out and vanishing again, quivered a little star, while a little further off the crescent of the moon shone white upon a background of azure, faintly flushed with red. I drew Vera Nikolaevna's attention to the cloud.

'Yes,' she said, 'that is lovely; but look in this direction.' I looked round. An immense dark-blue storm-cloud rose up, hiding the setting sun; it reared a crest like a thick sheaf flung upwards against the sky; it was surrounded by a bright rim of menacing purple, which in one place, in the very middle, broke right through its mighty mass, like fire from a burning crater.…

'There'll be a storm,' remarked Priemkov.

But I am wandering from the main point.

I forgot to tell you in my last letter that when I got home from the Priemkovs' I felt sorry I had mentioned *Faust*; Schiller would have been a great deal better for the first time, if it was to be something

German. I felt especially afraid of the first scenes, before the meeting with Gretchen. I was not quite easy about Mephistopheles either. But I was under the spell of *Faust*, and there was nothing else I could have read with zest. It was quite dark when we went into the summer-house; it had been made ready for us the day before. Just opposite the door, before a little sofa, stood a round table covered with a cloth; easy-chairs and seats were placed round it; there was a lamp alight on the table. I sat down on the little sofa, and took out the book. Vera Nikolaevna settled herself in an easy-chair, a little way off, close to the door. In the darkness, through the door, a green branch of acacia stood out in the lamplight, swaying lightly; from time to time a flood of night air flowed into the room. Priemkov sat near me at the table, the German beside him. The governess had remained in the house with Natasha. I made a brief, introductory speech. I touched on the old legend of doctor Faust, the significance of Mephistopheles, and Goethe himself, and asked them to stop me if anything struck them as obscure. Then I cleared my throat.... Priemkov asked me if I wouldn't have some sugar water, and one could perceive that he was very well satisfied with himself for having put this question to me. I refused. Profound silence reigned. I began to read, without raising my eyes. I felt ill at ease; my heart beat, and my voice shook. The first exclamation of sympathy came from the German, and he was the only one to break the silence all the

while I was reading.... 'Wonderful! sublime!' he repeated, adding now and then, 'Ah! that's profound.'
Priemkov, as far as I could observe, was bored; he did
not know German very well, and had himself admit-
ted he did not care for poetry!... Well, it was his own
doing! I had wanted to hint at dinner that his com-
pany could be dispensed with at the reading, but I felt
a delicacy about saying so. Vera Nikolaevna did not
stir; twice I stole a glance at her. Her eyes were fixed
directly and intently upon me; her face struck me as
pale. After the first meeting of Faust with Gretchen
she bent forward in her low chair, clasped her hands,
and remained motionless in that position till the end.
I felt that Priemkov was thoroughly sick of it, and at
first that depressed me, but gradually I forgot him,
warmed up, and read with fire, with enthusiasm.... I
was reading for Vera Nikolaevna alone; an inner voice
told me that *Faust* was affecting her. When I finished
(the intermezzo I omitted: that bit belongs in style to
the second part, and I skipped part, too, of the 'Night
on the Brocken') ... when I finished, when that last
'Heinrich!' was heard, the German with much feeling
commented—'My God! how splendid!' Priemkov,
apparently overjoyed (poor chap!), leaped up, gave a
sigh, and began thanking me for the treat I had given
them.... But I made him no reply; I looked towards
Vera Nikolaevna ... I wanted to hear what she would
say. She got up, walked irresolutely towards the door,
stood a moment in the doorway, and softly went out
into the garden. I rushed after her. She was already

some paces off; her dress was just visible, a white patch in the thick shadow.

'Well?' I called—'didn't you like it?'

She stopped.

'Can you leave me that book?' I heard her voice saying.

'I will present it you, Vera Nikolaevna, if you care to have it.'

'Thank you!' she answered, and disappeared.

Priemkov and the German came up to me.

'How wonderfully warm it is!' observed Priemkov; 'it's positively stifling. But where has my wife gone?'

'Home, I think,' I answered.

'I suppose it will soon be time for supper,' he rejoined. 'You read splendidly,' he added, after a short pause.

'Vera Nikolaevna liked *Faust*, I think,' said I.

'No doubt of it!' cried Priemkov.

'Oh, of course!' chimed in Schimmel.

We went into the house.

'Where's your mistress?' Priemkov inquired of a maid who happened to meet us.

'She has gone to her bedroom.'

Priemkov went off to her bedroom.

I went out on to the terrace with Schimmel. The old man raised his eyes towards the sky.

'How many stars!' he said slowly, taking a pinch of snuff; 'and all are worlds,' he added, and he took another pinch.

I did not feel it necessary to answer him, and

simply gazed upwards in silence. A secret uncertainty weighed upon my heart.... The stars, I fancied, looked down seriously at us. Five minutes later Priemkov appeared and called us into the dining-room. Vera Nikolaevna came in soon after. We sat down.

'Look at Verotchka,' Priemkov said to me.

I glanced at her.

'Well? don't you notice anything?'

I certainly did notice a change in her face, but I answered, I don't know why—

'No, nothing.'

'Her eyes are red,' Priemkov went on.

I was silent.

'Only fancy! I went upstairs to her and found her crying. It's a long while since such a thing has happened to her. I can tell you the last time she cried; it was when our Sasha died. You see what you have done with your *Faust*!' he added, with a smile.

'So you see now, Vera Nikolaevna,' I began, 'that I was right when——'

'I did not expect this,' she interrupted me; 'but God knows whether you are right. Perhaps that was the very reason my mother forbade my reading such books,—she knew——'

Vera Nikolaevna stopped.

'What did she know?' I asked. 'Tell me.'

'What for? I'm ashamed of myself, as it is; what did I cry for? But we'll talk about it another time. There was a great deal I did not quite understand.'

'Why didn't you stop me?'

'I understood all the words, and the meaning of them, but——'

She did not finish her sentence, and looked away dreamily. At that instant there came from the garden the sound of rustling leaves, suddenly fluttering in the rising wind. Vera Nikolaevna started and looked round towards the open window.

'I told you there would be a storm!' cried Priemkov. 'But what made you start like that, Verotchka?'

She glanced at him without speaking. A faint, far-off flash of lightning threw a mysterious light on her motionless face.

'It's all due to your *Faust*,' Priemkov went on. 'After supper we must all go to by-by.... Mustn't we, Herr Schimmel?'

'After intellectual enjoyment physical repose is as grateful as it is beneficial,' responded the kind-hearted German, and he drank a wine-glass of vodka.

Immediately after supper we separated. As I said good-night to Vera Nikolaevna I pressed her hand; her hand was cold. I went up to the room assigned to me, and stood a long while at the window before I undressed and got into bed. Priemkov's prediction was fulfilled; the storm came close, and broke. I listened to the roar of the wind, the patter and splash of the rain, and watched how the church, built close by, above the lake, at each flash of lightning stood out, at one moment black against a background of white, at the next white against a background of black, and then was swallowed up in the darkness again.... But my thoughts were far away. I kept thinking of Vera Nikolaevna, of what she would say to me when she had read *Faust* herself, I thought of her tears, remembered how she had listened....

The storm had long passed away, the stars came out, all was hushed around. Some bird I did not know sang different notes, several times in succession repeating the same phrase. Its clear, solitary voice rang out strangely in the deep stillness; and still I did not go to bed....

Next morning, earlier than all the rest, I was down in the drawing-room. I stood before the portrait of Madame Eltsov. 'Aha,' I thought, with a secret feeling of ironical triumph, 'after all, I have read your daughter a forbidden book!' All at once I fancied— you have most likely noticed that eyes *en face* always seem fixed straight on any one looking at a picture— but this time I positively fancied the old lady moved them with a reproachful look on me.

I turned round, went to the window, and caught sight of Vera Nikolaevna. With a parasol on her shoulder and a light white kerchief on her head, she was walking about the garden. I went out at once and said good-morning to her.

'I didn't sleep all night,' she said; 'my head aches; I came out into the air—it may go off.'

'Can that be the result of yesterday's reading?' I asked.

'Of course; I am not used to it. There are things in

your book I can't get out of my mind; I feel as though they were simply turning my head,' she added, putting her hand to her forehead.

'That's splendid,' I commented; 'but I tell you what I don't like—I'm afraid this sleeplessness and headache may turn you against reading such things.'

'You think so?' she responded, and she picked a sprig of wild jasmine as she passed. 'God knows! I fancy if one has once entered on that path, there is no turning back.'

She suddenly flung away the spray.

'Come, let us sit down in this arbour,' she went on; 'and please, until I talk of it of my own accord, don't remind me—of that book.' (She seemed afraid to utter the name *Faust*.)

We went into the arbour and sat down.

'I won't talk to you about *Faust*,' I began; 'but you will let me congratulate you and tell you that I envy you.'

'You envy me?'

'Yes; you, as I know you now, with your soul, have such delights awaiting you! There are great poets besides Goethe; Shakespeare, Schiller—and, indeed, our own Pushkin, and you must get to know him too.'

She did not speak, and drew in the sand with her parasol.

O, my friend, Semyon Nikolaitch! if you could have seen how sweet she was at that instant; pale almost to transparency, stooping forward a little, weary, inwardly perturbed—and yet serene as the sky! I talked, talked a long while, then ceased, and sat in silence watching her.... She did not raise her eyes, and went on drawing with her parasol and rubbing it out again. Suddenly we heard quick, childish steps; Natasha ran into the arbour. Vera Nikolaevna drew herself up, rose, and to my surprise she embraced her daughter with a sort of passionate tenderness.... That was not one of her ways. Then Priemkov made his appearance. Schimmel, that grey-haired but punctual innocent, had left before daybreak so as not to miss a lesson. We went in to morning tea.

But I am tired; it's high time to finish this letter. It's sure to strike you as foolish and confused. I feel confused myself. I'm not myself. I don't know what's the matter with me. I am continually haunted by a little room with bare walls, a lamp, an open door, the fragrance and freshness of the night, and there, near the door, an intent youthful face, light white garments.... I understand now why I wanted to marry her: I was not so stupid, it seems, before my stay in Berlin as I had hitherto supposed. Yes, Semyon Nikolaitch, your friend is in a curious frame of mind. All this I know will pass off ... and if it doesn't pass off,—well, what then? it won't pass off, and that's all. But any way I am well satisfied with myself; in the first place, I have spent an exquisite evening; and secondly, if I have awakened that soul, who can blame me? Old Madame Eltsov is nailed up on the wall, and must hold her peace. The old thing!... I don't know all the details of her life; but I know she ran away from her father's house; she was not half Italian for nothing, it seems. She wanted to keep her daughter secure ... we shall see.

I must put down my pen. You, jeering person, pray think what you like of me, only don't jeer at me in writing. You and I are old friends, and ought to spare each other. Good-bye!—

YOURS, P. B.

Fifth Letter

From the SAME to the SAME

M—— Village, *July 26, 1850.*

IT'S a long time since I wrote to you, dear Semyon Nicolaitch; more than a month, I think. I had enough to write about but I was overcome by laziness. To tell the truth, I have hardly thought of you all this time. But from your last letter to me I gather that you are drawing conclusions in regard to me, which are unjust, that is to say, not altogether just. You imagine I have fallen in love with Vera (I feel it awkward, somehow, to call her Vera Nikolaevna); you are wrong. Of course I see her often, I like her extremely ... indeed, who wouldn't like her? I should like to see you in my place. She's an exquisite creature! Rapid intuition, together with the inexperience of a child, clear common-sense, and an innate feeling for beauty, a continual striving towards the true and the lofty, and a comprehension of everything, even of the vicious, even of the ridiculous, a soft womanly charm brooding over all this like an angel's white wings.... But what's the use of words! We have read a great deal, we have talked a great deal together during this month. Reading with her is a delight such as I had never experienced before. You seem to be discovering new worlds. She never goes into ecstasies over anything; anything boisterous is distasteful to her; she is softly radiant all over when she likes anything, and her face wears such a noble and good—yes, good expression. From her earliest childhood Vera has not known what deceit was; she is accustomed to truth, it is the breath of her being, and so in poetry too, only what is true strikes her as natural; at once, without effort or difficulty, she recognises it as a familiar face ... a great privilege and happiness. One must give her mother credit for it. How many times have I thought, as I watched Vera—yes, Goethe was right, 'the good even in their obscure striving feel always where the true path lies.' There is only one thing annoying—her husband is always about the place. (Please don't laugh a senseless guffaw, don't sully our pure friendship, even in thought). He is about as capable of understanding poetry as I am of playing the flute, but he does not like to lag behind his wife, he wants to improve himself too. Sometimes she puts me out of patience herself; all of a sudden a mood comes over her; she won't read or talk, she works at her embroidery frame, busies herself with Natasha, or with the housekeeper, runs off all at once into the kitchen, or

simply sits with her hands folded looking out of the
window, or sets to playing 'fools' with the nurse.... I
have noticed at these times it doesn't do to bother
her; it's better to bide one's time till she comes up,
begins to talk or takes up a book. She has a great deal
of independence, and I am very glad of it. In the
days of our youth, do you remember, young girls
would sometimes repeat one's own words to one, as
they so well knew how, and one would be in ecstasies
over the echo, and possibly quite impressed by it,
till one realised what it meant? but this woman's ...
not so; she thinks for herself. She takes nothing on
trust; there's no overawing her with authority; she
won't begin arguing; but she won't give in either. We
have discussed *Faust* more than once; but, strange to
say, Gretchen she never speaks of, herself, she only
listens to what I say of her. Mephistopheles terrifies
her, not as the devil, but as 'something which may
exist in every man....' These are her own words. I
began trying to convince her that this 'something' is
what we call reflection; but she does not understand
the word reflection in its German sense; she only
knows the French 'refléxion', and is accustomed to
regarding it as useful. Our relations are marvellous!
From a certain point of view I can say that I have
a great influence over her, and am, as it were, edu-
cating her; but she too, though she is unaware of it
herself, is changing me for the better in many ways.
It's only lately, for instance—thanks to her—that I
have discovered what an immense amount of con-

ventional, rhetorical stuff there is in many fine and celebrated poetical works. What leaves her cold is at once suspect in my eyes. Yes, I have grown better, serener. One can't be near her, see her, and remain the man one was.

What will come of all this? you ask. I really believe—nothing. I shall pass my time very delightfully till September and then go away. Life will seem dark and dreary to me for the first months ... I shall get used to it. I know how full of danger is any tie whatever between a man and a young woman, how imperceptibly one feeling passes into another ... I should have had the strength to break it off, if I had not been sure that we were both perfectly undisturbed. It is true one day something queer passed between us. I don't know how or from what—I remember we had been reading *Oniegin*—I kissed her hand. She turned a little away, bent her eyes upon me (I have never seen such a look, except in her; there is dreaminess and intent attention in it, and a sort of sternness), ... suddenly flushed, got up and went away. I did not succeed in being alone with her that day. She avoided me, and for four mortal hours she played cards with her husband, the nurse, and the governess! Next morning she proposed a walk in the garden to me. We walked all through it, down to the lake. Suddenly without turning towards me, she softly whispered—'Please don't do that again!' and instantly began telling me about something else.... I was very much ashamed.

I must admit that her image is never out of my mind, and indeed I may almost say I have begun writing a letter to you with the object of having a reason for thinking and talking about her. I hear the tramp and neighing of horses; it's my carriage being got ready. I am going to see them. My coachman has given up asking me where to drive to, when I get into my carriage—he takes me straight off to the Priemkovs'. A mile and a half from their village, at an abrupt turn in the road, their house suddenly peeps out from behind a birch copse.... Each time I feel a thrill of joy in my heart directly I catch the glimmer of its windows in the distance. Schimmel (the harmless old man comes to see them from time to time; the princes H——, thank God, have only called once) ... Schimmel, with the modest solemnity characteristic of him, said very aptly, pointing to the house where Vera lives: 'That is the abode of peace!' In that house dwells an angel of peace....

> Cover me with thy wing,
> Still the throbbing of my heart,
> And grateful will be the shade
> To the enraptured soul....

But enough of this; or you'll be fancying all sorts of things. Till next time ... What shall I write to you next time, I wonder?—Good-bye! By the way, she never says 'Good-bye,' but always, 'So, good-bye!'—I like that tremendously.—

YOURS, P. B.

P.S.—I can't recollect whether I told you that she knows I wanted to marry her.

Sixth Letter

From the SAME to the SAME

M——— Village, *August 10, 1850.*

CONFESS you are expecting a letter from me of despair or of rapture!... Nothing of the sort. My letter will be like any other letter. Nothing new has happened, and nothing, I imagine, possibly can happen. The other day we went out in a boat on the lake. I will tell you about this boating expedition. We were three: she, Schimmel, and I. I don't know what induces her to invite the old fellow so often. The H———s, I hear, are annoyed with him for neglecting his lessons. This time, though, he was entertaining. Priemkov did not come with us; he had a headache. The weather was splendid, brilliant; great white clouds that seemed torn to shreds over a blue sky, everywhere glitter, a rustle in the trees, the plash and lapping of water on the bank, running coils of gold on the waves, freshness and sunlight! At first the German and I rowed; then we hoisted a sail and flew before the wind. The boat's bow almost dipped in the water, and a constant hissing and foaming followed the helm. She sat at the rudder and steered; she tied a kerchief over her head; she could not have kept a hat on; her curls strayed from under it and fluttered in the air. She held the rudder firmly in her little sunburnt hand, and smiled at the spray which flew at times in her face. I was curled up at the bottom of the boat; not far from her feet. The German brought out a pipe, smoked his shag, and, only fancy, began singing in a rather pleasing bass. First he sang the old-fashioned song: 'Freut euch des Lebens,' then an air from the 'Magic Flute,' then a song called the 'A B C of Love.' In this song all the letters of the alphabet—with additions of course—are sung through in order, beginning with 'A B C D—Wenn ich dich seh!' and ending with 'U V W X—Mach einen Knicks!' He sang all the couplets with much expression; but you should have seen how slily he winked with his left eye at the word 'Knicks!' Vera laughed and shook her finger at him. I observed that, as far as I could judge, Mr. Schimmel had been a re-doubtable fellow in his day. 'Oh yes, I could take my own part!' he rejoined with dignity; and he knocked the ash out of his pipe on to his open hand, and, with a knowing air, held the mouth-piece on one side in his teeth, while he felt in the tobacco-pouch. 'When I was a student,' he added, 'o-oh-oh!' He said nothing more. But what an o-oh-oh! it was! Vera begged him to sing some students' song, and he sang her: 'Knaster, den gelben,' but broke down on the last note. Alto-gether he was quite jovial and expansive. Meanwhile the wind had blown up, the waves began to be rather large, and the boat heeled a little over on one side; swallows began flitting above the water all about us. We made the sail loose and began to tack about. The wind suddenly blew a cross squall, we had not time to right the sail, a wave splashed over the boat's edge and flung a lot of water into the boat. And now the German proved himself a man of spirit; he snatched the cord from me, and set the sail right, saying as he did so—'So macht man ins Kuxhaven!'

Vera was most likely frightened, for she turned pale, but as her way is, she did not utter a word, but picked up her skirt, and put her feet upon the cross-piece of the boat. I was suddenly reminded of the poem of Goethe's (I have been simply steeped in him for some time past) ... you remember?—'On the waves glitter a thousand dancing stars,' and I repeated it aloud. When I reached the line: 'My eyes, why do you look down?' she slightly raised her eyes (I was sitting lower than she; her gaze had rested on me from above) and looked a long while away into the distance, screwing up her eyes from the wind.... A light rain came on in an instant, and pattered, making bubbles on the water. I offered her my overcoat; she put it over her shoulders. We got to the bank—not at the landing-place—and walked home. I gave her my arm. I kept feeling that I wanted to tell her something; but I did not speak. I asked her, though, I remember, why she always sat, when she was at home, under the portrait of Madame Eltsov, like a little bird under its mother's wing. 'Your comparison is a very true one,' she responded, 'I never want to come out from under her wing.' 'Shouldn't you like to come out into freedom?' I asked again. She made no answer.

I don't know why I have described this expedition
—perhaps, because it has remained in my memory as
one of the brightest events of the past days, though,
in reality, how can one call it an event? I had such a
sense of comfort and unspeakable gladness of heart,
and tears, light, happy tears were on the point of
bursting from my eyes.

Oh! fancy, the next day, as I was walking in the
garden by the arbour, I suddenly heard a pleasing,
musical, woman's voice singing—'Freut euch des
Lebens!...' I glanced into the arbour: it was Vera.
'Bravo!' I cried; 'I didn't know you had such a splendid voice.' She was rather abashed, and did not speak.
Joking apart, she has a fine, strong soprano. And I do
believe she has never even suspected that she has a
good voice. What treasures of untouched wealth lie
hid in her! She does not know herself. But am I not
right in saying such a woman is a rarity in our time?

August 12.

We had a very strange conversation yesterday. We
touched first upon apparitions. Fancy, she believes
in them, and says she has her own reasons for it.
Priemkov, who was sitting there, dropped his eyes,
and shook his head, as though in confirmation of her
words. I began questioning her, but soon noticed that
this conversation was disagreeable to her. We began
talking of imagination, of the power of imagination.
I told them that in my youth I used to dream a great
deal about happiness (the common occupation of
people, who have not had or are not having good

luck in life). Among other dreams, I used to brood over the bliss it would be to spend a few weeks, with the woman I loved, in Venice. I so often mused over this, especially at night, that gradually there grew up in my head a whole picture, which I could call up at will: I had only to close my eyes. This is what I imagined—night, a moon, the moonlight white and soft, a scent—of lemon, do you suppose? no, of vanilla, a scent of cactus, a wide expanse of water, a flat island overgrown with olives; on the island, at the edge of the shore, a small marble house, with open windows; music audible, coming from I know not where; in the house trees with dark leaves, and the light of a half-shaded lamp; from one window, a heavy velvet cloak, with gold fringe, hangs out with one end falling in the water; and with their arms on the cloak, sit *he* and *she*, gazing into the distance where Venice can be seen. All this rose as clearly before my mind as though I had seen it all with my own eyes. She listened to my nonsense, and said that she too often dreamed, but that her day-dreams were of a different sort: she fancied herself in the deserts of Africa, with some explorer, or seeking the traces of Franklin in the frozen Arctic Ocean. She vividly imagined all the hardships she had to endure, all the difficulties she had to contend with....

'You have read a lot of travels,' observed her husband.

'Perhaps,' she responded; 'but if one must dream, why need one dream of the unattainable?'

'And why not?' I retorted. 'Why is the poor unattainable to be condemned?'

'I did not say that,' she said; 'I meant to say, what need is there to dream of oneself, of one's own happiness? It's useless thinking of that; it does not come— why pursue it? It is like health; when you don't think of it, it means that it's there.'

These words astonished me. There's a great soul in this woman, believe me.... From Venice the conversation passed to Italy, to the Italians. Priemkov went away, Vera and I were left alone.

'You have Italian blood in your veins too,' I observed.

'Yes,' she responded; 'shall I show you the portrait of my grandmother?'

'Please do.'

She went to her own sitting-room, and brought out a rather large gold locket. Opening this locket, I saw excellently painted miniature portraits of Madame Eltsov's father and his wife—the peasant woman from Albano. Vera's grandfather struck me by his likeness to his daughter. Only his features, set in a white cloud of powder, seemed even more severe, sharp, and hard, and in his little yellow eyes there was a gleam of a sort of sullen obstinacy. But what a face the Italian woman had, voluptuous, open like a full-blown rose, with prominent, large, liquid eyes, and complacently smiling red lips! Her delicate sensual nostrils seemed dilating and quivering as after recent kisses. The dark cheeks seemed fragrant of glowing heat and health, the luxuriance of youth and womanly power.... That brow had never done any thinking, and, thank God, she had been depicted in her Albanian dress! The artist (a master) had put a vine in her hair, which was black as pitch with bright grey high lights; this Bacchic ornament was in marvellous keeping with the expression of her face. And do you know of whom the face reminded me? My Manon Lescaut in the black frame. And what is most wonderful of all, as I looked at the portrait, I recalled that in Vera too, in spite of the utter dissimilarity of the features, there is at times a gleam of something like that smile, that look....

Yes, I tell you again; neither she herself nor any one else in the world knows as yet all that is latent in her....

By the way—Madame Eltsov, before her daughter's marriage, told her all her life, her mother's death, and so on, probably with a view to her edification. What specially affected Vera was what she heard about her grandfather, the mysterious Ladanov. Isn't it owing to that that she believes in apparitions? It's strange! She is so pure and bright herself, and yet is afraid of everything dark and underground, and believes in it....

But enough. Why write all this? However, as it is written, it may be sent off to you.—

Yours, P. B.

Seventh Letter

From the SAME to the SAME

M—— Village, *August 22, 1850.*

I TAKE up my pen ten days after my last letter.... Oh my dear fellow, I can't hide my feelings any longer!... How wretched I am! How I love her! You can imagine with what a thrill of bitterness I write that fatal word. I am not a boy, not a young man even; I am no longer at that stage when to deceive another is almost impossible, but to deceive oneself costs no effort. I know all, and see clearly. I know that I am just on forty, that she's another man's wife, that she loves her husband; I know very well that the unhappy feeling which has gained possession of me can lead to nothing but secret torture and an utter waste of vital energy—I know all that, I expect nothing, and I wish for nothing; but I am not the better off for that. As long as a month ago I began to notice that the attraction she has for me was growing stronger and stronger. This partly troubled me, and partly even delighted me.... But how could I dream that everything would be repeated with me, which you would have thought could no more come again than youth can? What am I saying! I never loved like this, no, never! Manon Lescauts, Fritilions, these were my idols—such idols can easily be broken; but now ... only now, I have found out what it is to love a woman. I feel ashamed even to speak of it; but it's so. I'm ashamed.... Love is egoism any way; and at my years it's not permissible to be an egoist; at thirty-seven one cannot live for oneself; one must live to some purpose, with the aim of doing one's duty, one's work on earth. And I had begun to set to work.... And here everything is scattered to the winds again, as by a hurricane! Now I understand what I wrote to you in my first letter; I understand now what was the experience I had missed. How suddenly this blow has fallen upon me! I stand and look senselessly forward; a black veil hangs before my eyes; my heart is full of heaviness and dread! I can control myself, I am outwardly calm not only before others, but even in solitude. I can't really rave like a boy! But the worm has crept into my heart, and gnaws it night and day. How will it end? Hitherto I have fretted and suffered when away from her, and in her presence was at peace again at once—now I have no rest even when I am with her, that is what alarms me. Oh my friend, how hard it is to be ashamed of one's tears, to hide them! Only youth may weep; tears are only fitting for the young....

I cannot read over this letter; it has been wrung from me involuntarily, like a groan. I can add nothing, tell you nothing.... Give me time; I will come to myself, and possess my soul again; I will talk to you like a man, but now I am longing to lay my head on your breast and——

Oh Mephistopheles! you too are no help to me! I stopped short of set purpose, of set purpose I called up what irony is in me, I told myself how ludicrous and mawkish these laments, these outbursts will seem to me in a year, in half a year.... No, Mephistopheles is powerless, his tooth has lost its edge.... Farewell.—

YOURS, P. B.

Eighth Letter
From the SAME to the SAME

M—— Village, *September 8, 1850.*

MY DEAR SEMYON NIKOLAITCH,—You have taken my last letter too much to heart. You know I have always been given to exaggerating my sensations. It's done as it were unconsciously in me; a womanish nature! In the process of years this will pass away of course; but I admit with a sigh I have not corrected the failing so far. So set your mind at rest. I am not going to deny the impression made on me by Vera, but I say again, in all this there is nothing out of the way. For you to come here, as you write of doing, would be out of the question, quite. Post over a thousand versts, God knows with what object—why, it would be madness! But I am very grateful for this fresh proof of your affection, and believe me, I shall never forget it. Your journey here would be the more out of place as I mean to come to Petersburg shortly myself. When I am sitting on your sofa, I shall have a great deal to tell you, but now I really don't want to; what's the use? I shall only talk nonsense, I dare say, and muddle things up. I will write to you again before I start. And so good-bye for a little while. Be well and happy, and don't worry yourself too much about the fate of—

YOUR DEVOTED, P. B.

Ninth Letter
From the SAME to the SAME

P—— Village, *March 10, 1853.*

I HAVE been a long while without answering your letter; I have been all these days thinking about it. I felt that it was not idle curiosity but real friendship that prompted you, and yet I hesitated whether to follow your advice, whether to act on your desire. I have made up my mind at last; I will tell you everything. Whether my confession will ease my heart as you suppose, I don't know; but it seems to me I have no right to hide from you what has changed my life for ever; it seems to me, indeed, that I should be wronging—alas! even more wronging—the dear being ever in my thoughts, if I did not confide our mournful secret to the one heart still dear to me. You alone, perhaps, on earth, remember Vera, and you judge of her lightly and falsely; that I cannot endure. You shall know all. Alas! it can all be told in a couple of words. All there was between us flashed by in an instant, like lightning, and like lightning, brought death and ruin.... Over two years have passed since she died; since I took up my abode in this remote

51

spot, which I shall not leave till the end of my days, and everything is still as vivid in my memory, my wounds are still as fresh, my grief as bitter.... I will not complain. Complaints rouse up sorrow and so ease it, but not mine. I will begin my story.

Do you remember my last letter—the letter in which I tried to allay your fears and dissuaded you from coming from Petersburg? You suspected its assumed lightness of tone, you put no faith in our seeing each other soon; you were right. On the day before I wrote to you, I had learnt that I was loved. As I write these words, I realise how hard it would be for me to tell my story to the end. The ever insistent thought of her death will torture me with redoubled force, I shall be consumed by these memories.... But I will try to master myself, and will either throw aside the pen, or will say not a word more than is necessary. This is how I learnt that Vera loved me. First of all I must tell you (and you will believe me) that up to that day I had absolutely no suspicion. It is true she had grown pensive at times, which had never been the way with her before; but I did not know why this change had come upon her. At last, one day, the seventh of September—a day memorable for me— this is what happened. You know how I loved her and how wretched I was. I wandered about like an uneasy spirit, and could find no rest. I tried to keep at home, but I could not control myself, and went off to her. I found her alone in her own sitting-room. Priemkov was not at home, he had gone out shooting.

When I went in to Vera, she looked intently at me and did not respond to my bow. She was sitting at the window; on her knees lay a book I recognised at once; it was my *Faust*. Her face showed traces of weariness. I sat down opposite her. She asked me to read aloud the scene of Faust with Gretchen, when she asks him if he believes in God. I took the book and began reading. When I had finished, I glanced at her. Her head leaning on the back of her low chair and her arms crossed on her bosom, she was still looking as intently at me.

I don't know why, my heart suddenly began to throb.

'What have you done to me?' she said in a slow voice.

'What?' I articulated in confusion.

'Yes, what have you done to me?' she repeated.

'You mean to say,' I began; 'why did I persuade you to read such books?'

She rose without speaking, and went out of the room. I looked after her.

On the doorway she stopped and turned to me.

'I love you,' she said; 'that's what you have done to me.'

The blood rushed to my head....

'I love you, I am in love with you,' repeated Vera.

She went out and shut the door after her. I will not try to describe what passed within me then. I remember I went out into the garden, made my way into a thicket, leaned against a tree, and how long I stood there, I could not say. I felt faint and numb; a feeling of bliss came over my heart with a rush from time to time.... No, I cannot speak of that. Priemkov's voice roused me from my stupor; they had sent to tell him I had come: he had come home from shooting and was looking for me. He was surprised at finding me alone in the garden, without a hat on, and he led me into the house. 'My wife's in the drawing-room,' he observed; 'let's go to her.' You can imagine my sensations as I stepped through the doorway of the drawing-room. Vera was sitting in the corner, at her embroidery frame; I stole a glance at her, and it was a long while before I raised my eyes again. To my amazement, she seemed composed; there was no trace of agitation in what she said, nor in the sound of her voice. At last I brought myself to look at her. Our eyes met.... She faintly blushed, and bent over her canvas. I began to watch her. She seemed, as it were, perplexed; a cheerless smile hung about her lips now and then.

Priemkov went out. She suddenly raised her head and in a rather loud voice asked me—'What do you intend to do now?'

I was taken aback, and hurriedly, in a subdued voice, answered, that I intended to do the duty of an honest man—to go away, 'for,' I added, 'I love you, Vera Nikolaevna, you have probably seen that long ago.' She bent over her canvas again and seemed to ponder.

'I must talk with you,' she said; 'come this evening

after tea to our little house ... you know, where you read *Faust*.'

She said this so distinctly that I can't to this day conceive how it was Priemkov, who came into the room at that instant, heard nothing. Slowly, terribly slowly, passed that day. Vera sometimes looked about her with an expression as though she were asking herself if she were not dreaming. And at the same time there was a look of determination in her face; while I ... I could not recover myself. Vera loves me! These words were continually going round and round in my head; but I did not understand them— I neither understood myself nor her. I could not believe in such unhoped-for, such overwhelming happiness; with an effort I recalled the past, and I too looked and talked as in a dream....

After evening tea, when I had already begun to think how I could steal out of the house unobserved, she suddenly announced of her own accord that she wanted a walk, and asked me to accompany her. I got up, took my hat, and followed her. I did not dare begin to speak, I could scarcely breathe, I awaited her first word, I awaited explanations; but she did not speak. In silence we reached the summer-house, in silence we went into it, and then—I don't know to this day, I can't understand how it happened— we suddenly found ourselves in each other's arms. Some unseen force flung me to her and her to me. In the fading daylight, her face, with the curls tossed back, lighted up for an instant with a smile of self-surrender and tenderness, and our lips met in a kiss....

That kiss was the first and last.

Vera suddenly broke from my arms and with an expression of horror in her wide open eyes staggered back——

'Look round,' she said in a shaking voice; 'do you see nothing?'

I turned round quickly.

'Nothing. Why, do you see something?'

'Not now, but I did.'

She drew deep, gasping breaths.

'Whom? what?'

'My mother,' she said slowly, and she began trembling all over. I shivered too, as though with cold. I suddenly felt ashamed, as though I were guilty. And indeed, wasn't I guilty at that instant?

'Nonsense!' I began; 'what do you mean? Tell me rather——'

'No, for God's sake, no!' she interposed, clutching her head. 'This is madness—I'm going out of my mind.... One can't play with this—it's death.... Good-bye....'

I held out my hands to her.

'Stay, for God's sake, for an instant,' I cried in an involuntary outburst. I didn't know what I was saying and could scarcely stand upright. 'For God's sake ... it is too cruel!'

She glanced at me.

'To-morrow, to-morrow evening,' she said, 'not to-day, I beseech you—go away to-day ... to-morrow evening come to the garden gate, near the lake. I will be there, I will come.... I swear to you I will come,' she added with passion, and her eyes shone; 'whoever may hinder me, I swear! I will tell you everything, only let me go to-day.'

And before I could utter a word she was gone. Utterly distraught, I stayed where I was. My head was in a whirl. Across the mad rapture, which filled my whole being, there began to steal a feeling of apprehension.... I looked round. The dim, damp room in which I was standing oppressed me with its low roof and dark walls.

I went out and walked with dejected steps towards the house. Vera was waiting for me on the terrace; she went into the house directly I drew near, and at once retreated to her bedroom.

I went away.

How I spent the night and the next day till the evening I can't tell you. I only remember that I lay, my face hid in my hands, I recalled her smile before our kiss, I whispered—'At last, she....'

I recalled, too, Madame Eltsov's words, which Vera had repeated to me. She had said to her once, 'You are like ice; until you melt as strong as stone, but directly you melt there's nothing of you left.'

Another thing recurred to my mind; Vera and I had once been talking of talent, ability.

'There's only one thing I can do,' she said; 'keep silent till the last minute.'

I did not understand it in the least at the time.

'But what is the meaning of her fright?' I wondered—'Can she really have seen Madame Eltsov? Imagination!' I thought, and again I gave myself up to the emotions of expectation.

It was on that day I wrote you,—with what thoughts in my head it hurts me to recall—that deceitful letter.

In the evening—the sun had not yet set—I took up my stand about fifty paces from the garden gate in a tall thicket on the edge of the lake. I had come from home on foot. I will confess to my shame; fear, fear of the most cowardly kind, filled my heart; I was incessantly starting ... but I had no feeling of remorse. Hiding among the twigs, I kept continual watch on the little gate. It did not open. The sun set, the evening drew on; then the stars came out, and the sky turned black. No one appeared. I was in a fever. Night came on. I could bear it no longer; I came cautiously out of the thicket and stole down to the gate. Everything was still in the garden. I called Vera, in a whisper, called a second time, a third.... No voice called back. Half-an-hour more passed by, and an hour; it became quite dark. I was worn out by suspense; I drew the gate towards me, opened it at once, and on tiptoe, like a thief, walked towards the house. I stopped in the shadow of a lime-tree.

Almost all the windows in the house had lights in them; people were moving to and fro in the house. This surprised me; my watch, as far as I could make out in the dim starlight, said half-past eleven. Suddenly I heard a noise near the house; a carriage drove out of the courtyard.

'Visitors, it seems,' I thought. Losing every hope of seeing Vera, I made my way out of the garden and walked with rapid steps homewards. It was a dark September night, but warm and windless. The feeling, not so much of annoyance as of sadness, which had taken possession of me, gradually disappeared, and I got home, rather tired from my rapid walk, but soothed by the peacefulness of the night, happy and almost light-hearted. I went to my room, dismissed Timofay, and without undressing, flung myself on my bed and plunged into reverie.

At first my day-dreams were sweet, but soon I noticed a curious change in myself. I began to feel a sort of secret gnawing anxiety, a sort of deep, inward uneasiness. I could not understand what it arose from, but I began to feel sick and sad, as though I were menaced by some approaching trouble, as though some one dear to me were suffering at that instant and calling on me for help. A wax candle on the table burnt with a small, steady flame, the pendulum swung with a heavy, regular tick. I leant my head on my hand and fell to gazing into the empty half-dark of my lonely room. I thought of Vera, and my heart failed me; all, at which I had so rejoiced, struck me, as it ought to have done, as unhappiness, as hopeless ruin. The feeling of apprehension grew and grew; I could not lie still any longer; I suddenly fancied again that some one was calling me in a voice of entreaty.... I raised my head and shuddered; I had not been mistaken; a pitiful cry floated out of the distance and rang faintly resounding on the dark window-panes. I was frightened; I jumped off the bed; I opened the window. A distinct moan broke into the room and, as it were, hovered about me. Chilled with terror, I drank in its last dying echoes. It seemed as though some one were being killed in the distance and the luckless wretch were beseeching in vain for mercy. Whether it was an owl hooting in the wood or some other creature that uttered this wail, I did not think to consider at the time, but, like Mazeppa, I called back in answer to the ill-omened sound.

'Vera, Vera!' I cried; 'is it you calling me?' Timofay, sleepy and amazed, appeared before me.

I came to my senses, drank a glass of water, and went into another room; but sleep did not come to me. My heart throbbed painfully though not rapidly. I could not abandon myself to dreams of happiness again; I dared not believe in it.

Next day, before dinner, I went to the Priemkovs'. Priemkov met me with a care-worn face.

'My wife is ill,' he began; 'she is in bed; I sent for a doctor.'

'What is the matter with her?'

'I can't make out. Yesterday evening she went into the garden and suddenly came back quite beside herself, panic-stricken. Her maid ran for me. I went in, and asked my wife what was wrong. She made no answer, and so she has lain; by night delirium set in. In her delirium she said all sorts of things; she mentioned you. The maid told me an extraordinary thing; that Vera's mother appeared to her in the garden; she fancied she was coming to meet her with open arms.'

You can imagine what I felt at these words.

'Of course that's nonsense,' Priemkov went on; 'though I must admit that extraordinary things have happened to my wife in that way.'

'And you say Vera Nikolaevna is very unwell?'

'Yes: she was very bad in the night; now she is wandering.'

'What did the doctor say?'

'The doctor said that the disease was undefined as yet....'

March 12.

I cannot go on as I began, dear friend; it costs me too much effort and re-opens my wounds too cruelly. The disease, to use the doctor's words, became defined, and Vera died of it. She did not live a fortnight after the fatal day of our momentary interview. I saw her once more before her death. I have no memory more heart-rending. I had already learned from the doctor that there was no hope. Late in the evening, when every one in the house was in bed, I stole to the door of her room and looked in at her. Vera lay in her bed, with closed eyes, thin and small, with a feverish flush on her cheeks. I gazed at her as though turned to stone. All at once she opened her eyes, fastened them upon me, scrutinised me, and stretching out a wasted hand—

'Was will er an dem heiligen Ort
Der da ... der dort[1]

she articulated, in a voice so terrible that I rushed
headlong away. Almost all through her illness, she
raved about *Faust* and her mother, whom she sometimes called Martha, sometimes Gretchen's mother.

Vera died. I was at her burying. Ever since then
I have given up everything and am settled here for
ever.

Think now of what I have told you; think of her,
of that being so quickly brought to destruction. How
it came to pass, how explain this incomprehensible
intervention of the dead in the affairs of the living, I
don't know and never shall know. But you must admit
that it is not a fit of whimsical spleen, as you express
it, which has driven me to retire from the world. I am
not what I was, as you knew me; I believe in a great
deal now which I did not believe formerly. All this
time I have thought so much of that unhappy woman
(I had almost said, girl), of her origin, of the secret
play of fate, which we in our blindness call blind
chance. Who knows what seeds each man living on
earth leaves behind him, which are only destined
to come up after his death? Who can say by what
mysterious bond a man's fate is bound up with his
children's, his descendants'; how his yearnings are
reflected in them, and how they are punished for his
errors? We must all submit and bow our heads before
the Unknown.

---

[1]*Faust*, Part I., Last Scene.

Yes, Vera perished, while I was untouched. I remember, when I was a child, we had in my home a lovely vase of transparent alabaster. Not a spot sullied its virgin whiteness. One day when I was left alone, I began shaking the stand on which it stood ... the vase suddenly fell down and broke to shivers. I was numb with horror, and stood motionless before the fragments. My father came in, saw me, and said, 'There, see what you have done; we shall never have our lovely vase again; now there is no mending it!' I sobbed. I felt I had committed a crime.

I grew into a man—and thoughtlessly broke a vessel a thousand times more precious....

In vain I tell myself that I could not have dreamed of such a sudden catastrophe, that it struck me too with its suddenness, that I did not even suspect what sort of nature Vera was. She certainly knew how to be silent till the last minute. I ought to have run away directly I felt that I loved her, that I loved a married woman. But I stayed, and that fair being was shattered, and with despair I gaze at the work of my own hands.

Yes, Madame Eltsov took jealous care of her daughter. She guarded her to the end, and at the first incautious step bore her away with her to the grave!

It is time to make an end.... I have not told one hundredth part of what I ought to have; but this has been enough for me. Let all that has flamed up fall back again into the depths of my heart.... In conclusion, I say to you—one conviction I have gained from the experience of the last years—life is not jest and not amusement; life is not even enjoyment ... life is hard labour. Renunciation, continual renunciation—that is its secret meaning, its solution. Not the fulfilment of cherished dreams and aspirations, however lofty they may be—the fulfilment of duty, that is what must be the care of man. Without laying on himself chains, the iron chains of duty, he cannot reach without a fall the end of his career. But in youth we think—the freer the better, the further one will get. Youth may be excused for thinking so. But it is shameful to delude oneself when the stern face of truth has looked one in the eyes at last.

Good-bye! In old days I would have added, be happy; now I say to you, try to live, it is not so easy as it seems. Think of me, not in hours of sorrow, but in hours of contemplation, and keep in your heart the image of Vera in all its pure stainlessness.... Once more, good-bye!—

YOURS, P. B.

1855.

A NOTE ON LITERATURE

L ITERATURE, like any other art, is singularly interesting to the artist; and, in a degree peculiar to
itself among the arts, it is useful to mankind. These
are the sufficient justifications for any young man or
woman who adopts it as the business of his life. I
shall not say much about the wages. A writer can live
by his writing. If not so luxuriously as by other trades,
then less luxuriously. The nature of the work he does
all day will more affect his happiness than the quality
of his dinner at night. Whatever be your calling, and
however much it brings you in the year, you could
still, you know, get more by cheating. We all suffer
ourselves to be too much concerned about a little
poverty; but such considerations should not move
us in the choice of that which is to be the business
and justification of so great a portion of our lives;
and like the missionary, the patriot, or the philoso-
pher, we should all choose that poor and brave career
in which we can do the most and best for mankind.
Now Nature, faithfully followed, proves herself a care-
ful mother. A lad, for some liking to the jingle of
words, betakes himself to letters for his life; by-and-
by, when he learns more gravity, he finds that he has
chosen better than he knew; that if he earns little, he
is earning it amply; that if he receives a small wage,
he is in a position to do considerable services; that it
is in his power, in some small measure, to protect the
oppressed and to defend the truth. So kindly is the

world arranged, such great profit may arise from a small degree of human reliance on oneself, and such, in particular, is the happy star of this trade of writing, that it should combine pleasure and profit to both parties, and be at once agreeable, like fiddling, and useful, like good preaching.

GEOFFREY CHAUCER

BEN JONSON

SIR PHILLIP SIDNEY

EDMUND SPENSER

•   •   •   •   •   •   •

Man is imperfect; yet, in his literature, he must express himself and his own views and preferences; for to do anything else is to do a far more perilous thing than to risk being immoral: it is to be sure of being untrue. To ape a sentiment, even a good one, is to travesty a sentiment; that will not be helpful.

To conceal a sentiment, if you are sure you hold it, is to take a liberty with truth. There is probably no point of view possible to a sane man but contains some truth and, in the true connection, might be profitable to the race. I am not afraid of the truth, if any one could tell it me, but I am afraid of parts of it impertinently uttered. There is a time to dance and a time to mourn; to be harsh as well as to be sentimental; to be ascetic as well as to glorify the appetites; and if a man were to combine all these extremes into his work, each in its place and proportion, that work would be the world's masterpiece of morality as well as of art. Partiality is immorality; for any book is wrong that gives a misleading picture of the world and life. The trouble is that the weakling must be partial; the work of one proving dank and depressing; of another, cheap and vulgar; of a third, epileptically sensual; of a fourth, sourly ascetic. In literature as in conduct, you can never hope to do exactly right. All you can do is to make as sure as possible; and for that there is but one rule. Nothing should be done in a hurry that can be done slowly. It is no use to write a book and put it by for nine or even ninety years; for in the writing you will have partly convinced yourself; the delay must precede any beginning; and if you meditate a work of art, you should first long roll the subject under the tongue to make sure you like the flavour, before you brew a volume that shall taste of it from end to end; or if you propose to enter on the field of controversy, you should first have thought upon the question under all conditions, in health as well as in sickness, in sorrow as well as in joy. It is this nearness of examination necessary for any true and kind writing, that makes the practice of the art a prolonged and noble education for the writer.

JOHN DRYDEN

FRANCIS BACON

JOSEPH ADDISON

JONATHAN SWIFT

There is plenty to do, plenty to say, or to say over again, in the meantime. Any literary work which conveys faithful facts or pleasing impressions is a service to the public. It is even a service to be thankfully proud of having rendered. The slightest novels are a blessing to those in distress, not chloroform itself a greater. Our fine old sea-captain's life was justified when Carlyle soothed his mind with *The King's Own* or *Newton Forster*. To please is to serve; and so far from its being difficult to instruct while you amuse, it is difficult to do the one thoroughly without the other. Some part of the writer or his life will crop out in even a vapid book; and to read a novel that was conceived with any force is to multiply experience and to exercise the sympathies.

ALEXANDER POPE

ROBERT BURNS

SAMUEL JOHNSON

OLIVER GOLDSMITH

Every article, every piece of verse, every essay, every *entre-filet*, is destined to pass, however swiftly, through the minds of some portion of the public, and to colour, however transiently, their thoughts. When any subject falls to be discussed, some scribbler on a paper has the invaluable opportunity of beginning its discussion in a dignified and human spirit; and if there were enough who did so in our public press, neither the public nor the Parliament would find it in their minds to drop to meaner thoughts. The writer has the chance to stumble, by the way, on something pleasing, something interesting, something encouraging, were it only to a single reader. He will be unfortunate, indeed, if he suit no one. He has the chance, besides, to stumble on something that a dull person shall be able to comprehend; and for a dull person to have read anything and, for that once, comprehended it, makes a marking epoch in his education.

Here, then, is work worth doing and worth trying to do well. And so, if I were minded to welcome any great accession to our trade, it should not be from any reason of a higher wage, but because it was a trade which was useful in a very great and in a very high degree; which every honest tradesman could make more serviceable to mankind in his single strength; which was difficult to do well and possible to do better every year; which called for scrupulous thought on the part of all who practised it, and hence became a perpetual education to their nobler natures; and which, pay it as you please, in the large majority of the best cases will still be underpaid. For surely, at this time of day in the nineteenth century, there is nothing that an honest man should fear more timorously than getting and spending more than he deserves.

CHARLES DICKENS

THOMAS CARLYLE

The most influential books, and the truest in their influence, are works of fiction. They do not pin the reader to a dogma, which he must afterwards discover to be inexact; they do not teach him a lesson, which he must afterwards unlearn. They repeat, they rearrange, they clarify the lessons of life; they disengage us from ourselves, they constrain us to the acquaintance of others; and they show us the web of experience, not as we can see it for ourselves, but with a singular change—that monstrous, consuming *ego* of ours being, for the nonce, struck out. To be so, they must be reasonably true to the human comedy; and any work that is so serves the turn of instruction. But the course of our education is answered best by those poems and romances where we breathe a magnanimous atmosphere of thought and meet generous and pious characters.

WM. M. THACKERAY   GEORGE ELIOT

Excerpt from *Essays in the Art of Writing* by R. L. Stevenson.

Made in United States
North Haven, CT
22 January 2024

47779671R00046